I0623083

TALES OF TERROR

VOLUME 1

ETHAN HAYES

FREE REIGN

FREE REIGN
Publishing

CONTENTS_

COMING SOON!_

STALKED is a gripping and deeply personal compilation of firsthand accounts, where individuals bravely recount their harrowing experiences of being stalked. This powerful anthology grants readers intimate access to the voices of those who have endured the torment of stalking. Each account is a unique and unfiltered testimonial, allowing readers to step into the shoes of the victims themselves and experience the chilling events that unfolded in their lives.

Through these firsthand stories, readers will encounter individuals from diverse backgrounds, all united by the common thread of being stalked. From ordinary people to public figures, the accounts delve into the psychological, emotional, and physical toll inflicted by relentless pursuers.

With raw and unvarnished honesty, each narrator recounts the emotional rollercoaster of fear, anxiety, and trauma experienced during their ordeals. The stories not only expose the psychological manipulation and tactics employed by stalkers but also offer insights into the victims' journeys of survival, healing, and finding strength in the face of adversity.

Prepare to be moved and inspired as you immerse yourself in the deeply personal and unfiltered stories of survival in "Stalked," a compilation that amplifies the voices of those who have endured the unimaginable, while shedding light on the urgent need for societal change and support for victims of stalking.

CHAPTER ONE_
STRANGE SWAMP CREATURE

WHEN I WAS twenty-five years old in the 1980s, I decided to leave the home and town I grew up in and travel halfway across the country because I wanted to see what was out there. I was a bored, entitled know it all and thought that much more happiness could and would be had if I could just escape the small town I grew up in and the people in it. This little experiment of me living halfway across the country and on my own was funded solely by my parents and before I go any further, I would like to say that I eventually ended up back in that small town, reunited with my small-town friends and living very close to my parents. I married someone I went to high school with when I was thirty and still live there today. I thought I should put that in there because it always looks bad on me when I explain what I was doing halfway across the country at a remote wilderness area in the first place and I think it's important that people hear and pay attention to what happened to me out there. My parents knew someone who knew someone who knew about a little community in Florida that was made up of about fifteen cabins, all inside of a gated community in the middle of nowhere and surrounded by dense forested land, where they had an opening for a tenant. The cabins were tiny but I thought that anywhere was better than where I was and so I jumped at the opportunity to go out there and start my new life. I couldn't even see past my own ego and wild dreams to understand how dangerous it could get for me out there all alone as a young woman traveling at that time. My parents expressed their concerns, but I was only worried about them keeping the money in my bank account. I promised to start looking for a job as soon as I got out to Florida, and I left on a random Tuesday afternoon. I flew there and took a taxicab to the little community, and it should have been my first clue that something was wrong when the driver of the cab refused to drive me into the place itself and instead insisted that I pay him and get out at the gate. I didn't know where I was going. I just knew that the woman renting me the cabin was named Julia and she was waiting for me to get there in the welcome building. I was annoyed but did as the driver asked.

I grabbed all my belongings, which weren't many, and told the person at the gate who I was and why I was there. The man behind the gate suspiciously eyed the taxi and its driver until they were no longer within our sight and then he made a phone call, whispering the entire time, to who I assume was the woman I was out there to meet that day. He opened the gate and gave me directions on how to get to Julia's building. I was creeped out from the moment that taxi driver made me get out of his car, but I was out there to not only prove to myself that I could make it on my own but to also prove that same thing to my parents and anyone else I thought didn't think that I could. I took a deep breath, thanked him, and started walking uphill. There was nothing at all around but the road in front of me and deep woods all around me. It was dusk and I felt like something, or someone was watching me from the woods. I walked for almost twenty minutes before reaching my destination and a woman named Julia came out of the front door as I was still approaching it. She introduced herself and then we walked another mile or so to the cabin I was going to be renting. It was small but fully furnished. I asked her about all the other cabins and my neighbors, and she gave me a funny look. She told me, in a somewhat aggressive tone, that everyone there kept to themselves and that she and they would all appreciate it if I did the same. I was uncomfortable so I didn't hear much after that, but I did agree to not bother anyone or anything like that. Eventually she handed me my keys and briskly walked out of the cabin. She turned around to tell me to stay out of the woods at nighttime and to be especially careful of going near the swamp which, it turns out, my cabin was the closest to.

I had a stress headache by the time she left and just wanted to unpack my meager belongings and take a shower before bed. I picked up the landline phone to call my parents and tell them that I had made it okay and that I would be in touch with them. There was no dial tone, and I slammed the phone down. I was angry because I didn't want to have to survive without a phone. Julia told me how to get to her cabin in case I needed anything, and she also left me her phone number, but the number wouldn't do me any good at that point. I had just about had it with all the weirdness and decided that I could just walk to her cabin and ask her about the phone. Maybe she had one that I could use for the time being because I had promised my parents, I would let them know I made it okay. We didn't have cell phones and so they hadn't heard from me since the night before when I left their house and took a cab to the airport. I figured it couldn't have been that far and so I grabbed a flashlight and started walking. I carried the directions she gave me so that I could follow them and get to her cabin as quickly as possible. I was hoping I wouldn't have to trek through the woods all alone on the way back and that maybe she would take pity on me and offer me a ride. I didn't see anyone else or hear anyone either, for the first fifteen minutes I had been walking. I was out of breath and very agitated because she said she lived close by. I shined my flashlight on the map she had given me and realized I had somehow become lost. I was scared more than anything else and that's mainly because I hadn't ever spent much time in the woods and especially not at nighttime. There was a large rock that I sat down on as I tried to catch my breath and think for a minute. The phone obviously didn't seem that important anymore and all I wanted to do was get back to my cabin. I knew I needed to turn around but the whole forest looked the same and I had made more than a few turns to get to where I was. I thought the map was telling me to turn around and go left to get back on one of the trails that led back to my cabin and so that's the way I went. It took only walking that way for a couple of minutes before it became a dead end, and I was standing in front of the swamp.

I assumed that it was the same swamp I had been warned to stay away from and didn't know what to do except cry at that point. I tried calling out for help but all I heard in response was my own echo coming back to me through the trees and wilderness. I looked at the map again and finally realized where I had turned wrong, and I suddenly became confident that I knew where I was going. It was a relief, but it didn't last very long. As soon as I turned around and took no more than three steps, I heard a growling sound coming from behind me. I thought at first that I was hearing things, but I also suddenly felt like someone was behind me and staring right at my back. You know how it is when you just know that someone is behind you? That's how it felt, and I figured if they were friendly or someone willing to help, they would have been talking by that point and all I had heard was a growl. I suddenly heard a strange and headache inducing buzzing sound that seemed to be coming from all around me. I started getting very dizzy, but I put my hands over my ears to try and block out the noise. It was horrible and even though my ears recognized it as buzzing, it made me feel like I had always felt when I would hear sharp nails on a chalkboard. I became dizzy and nauseous and leaned back against a tree to stay balanced. I had my eyes closed and felt like I was going to faint and when I looked over, I saw something terrifying that I will never forget. The minute our eyes met the strange and very high-pitched sound stopped and there seemed to be no noise at all. In a forest, it's unnatural for there to not be any noise whatsoever and it made the whole situation so much more terrifying than it already was.

The creature had to have weighed at least three hundred and fifty pounds. It stood at around ten or eleven feet tall and looked like it had scales. It literally looked as though a crocodile got out of the swamp and stood up on its hind legs. The only difference was it had a regular, human sized head that was also the same shape as a human being's head. I just stared at it, and I think I was too shocked and scared to move or say anything. It looked at me with its glowing yellow eyes and eventually it smiled at me, revealing a mouth full of razor-sharp teeth. I didn't dare raise my flashlight to it at first and even without doing so I could plainly see that it was a female, whatever it was. It had body parts that looked like some that only human women have, including breasts and when it licked its lips, I got chills all over my body. I was already crying but I started to scream at the top of my lungs. Once again there was no response but my own echo. The creature kept looking like it wanted to come towards me, but something was holding it back. I shined the light on it, hoping it would just go away. It didn't leave altogether but it did recoil in anger and let out an even more ferocious growl, aimed in my direction. That's when I saw it had some sort of metal bar around its neck that seemed to have been attached to a metal chain. It turned its head at the sight of the light and the chains rattled. It was a leash! That thing was on a leash! I shined the flashlight out beyond the creature and into the swamp and I saw what looked like the silhouette of a human being standing there and holding something. A woman's voice, thickly accented, yelled for me to get the hell out of there and don't come back. That's just what I did.

I didn't know how to get back to my own cabin, but it turns out I didn't need to because I randomly ran into Julia while running for my life. She looked surprised and asked me what I was doing out there. I was hysterical and stammered out something about the phone and a lizard woman and humans with leashes. I couldn't form a proper sentence and of course I sounded like an absolute lunatic to any normal human being. She looked concerned but she somewhat chuckled at what I was saying and kept insisting I had somehow fallen asleep and had a nightmare. It didn't escape my notice though that as she led me away and towards my cabin, she kept looking behind us, towards the swamp, and she looked very nervous. We got back to my cabin, and she told me she would have someone come and look at the phone the next day and that I should get some rest. She reiterated her initial warning to stay to myself, stay out of the woods at night and to especially steer clear of the swamp at all times, no matter what. I asked her to elaborate on that, but she said she would at another time and that I obviously needed a shower and some sleep. She wasn't wrong. I called my parents the next day, but I told them that everything was fine. Eventually I got a job and moved out of the cabin around two years after I had initially moved in. I lived in fear the whole time I was there, and I never did get those answers from Miss Julia. I also never got to know any of my neighbors in that community and I almost never even saw any of them, no for the whole time I lived there. It was all very creepy, and I never really talked about it much. However, with all the news the last two decades or so about reptilians from other planets coming to earth and trying to take over our world and our elite, I thought it was a good time to start getting my story out there. I don't have any other information, but I do have a few more strange encounters. I never saw any other actual entities though, but I am quite sure, based on those other experiences, that there were more than a few terrifying, unnatural, and downright strange entities and creatures on that land and that most if not all the human beings who lived there knew all about what was going on. I didn't want to know back then but now I think I am ready for some answers. Thanks for letting me share this.

CHAPTER TWO_
SKINWALKER IN THE OZARKS

I HAD ALWAYS BEEN FASCINATED by the Ozarks. The rolling hills, the dense forests, and the winding rivers all held a certain magic that called to me. So, when I graduated high school and was accepted into college, I knew that I wanted to spend my summer exploring the wilderness. I packed my backpack with all the essentials - a tent, a sleeping bag, a map, and some food - and set out into the woods. I didn't have a specific destination in mind; I just wanted to wander and see where the trails would take me.

The first few days were magical. I hiked through fields of wildflowers, swam in crystal clear streams, and slept under the stars. It was everything I had hoped it would be. But then, on the third night, something changed. I had set up camp in a clearing near a small creek, and as I was drifting off to sleep, I heard whispers all around me. It was crazy but they had sounded like my mother. At first, I thought it was just my imagination playing tricks on me. But as the whispers grew louder and more insistent, I began to feel uneasy.

I called out for my mom - even though she was miles away - hoping that someone would hear me and come to my rescue. But no one answered. And then, out of nowhere, a figure appeared in front of me. It was tall and thin, with long arms and legs that seemed to stretch on forever. Long claws reached out gripping the trees to make marks that I felt would soon meet my own flesh. Its eyes glowed in the darkness, and its mouth twisted into a grotesque smile. Its limbs cracked like dry wood on a fire. It twisted with arms akimbo as if it was a living tree.

I knew then that I was face-to-face with a skin walker. I couldn't believe my eyes. The sheer horror froze my limbs, but I quickly snapped myself out of it. I didn't hesitate. I grabbed my backpack and ran as fast as I could out of the clearing and into the woods. I could hear the crackling woods behind me as the creature gave chase. It keeps calling my name as my mother and somehow that made it worse. I felt its claws reach out to me touching tendrils of my hair as if it was just teasing me with a touch to show its power.

I didn't stop running until I reached my car. I paused

and looked around to the woods and there was nothing but silence. And even then, I didn't feel safe. I knew that the skin walker could be anywhere, watching me, waiting for its chance to strike. It wasn't just your run of the mil cryptid; it was one that possessed supernatural powers. Did that mean it could somehow find me? If it ever chooses to, how could I keep myself safe? Would I spend the rest of my life in fear. Every night I would dream of those glowing red eyes and claws finding me. I would dream that it stood at the end of my bed drinking the fear out of me and laughing my mother's laugh.

Needless to say, this experience changed me. It made me realize that there was so much more to the world than what I had previously thought. And it inspired me to study behavioral psychology in college - to try and understand why people believe in things like skin walkers and other supernatural beings.

Years later, I'm still fascinated by the Ozarks and the mysteries that lie within. But now, I approach them with caution and respect, knowing that there are things out there that we may never fully understand. And that was not an option for me. I couldn't just let my fear dictate me. So, I made a few new lifestyle choices. After that encounter, I became obsessed with learning more about skin walkers and other supernatural beings. I spent countless hours researching Native American folklore and studying the psychology behind belief in the paranormal. I knew that as I learned more, I would never be caught unaware again. But most importantly I would never be a victim again.

I realized a lifelong passion then. Even though I got into it to for survival reasons, The folklore here was too rich to deny. Eventually, I realized that my fascination with the Ozarks was not just about the natural beauty of the region - it was also about the stories and legends that had been passed down through generations. I decided to add a double major with folklore. I wanted to understand what I experienced.

I talked to park rangers, historians, and members of Native American tribes who had lived in the area for centuries. Through these conversations, I learned about other creatures that were said to inhabit the Ozarks - like the Ozark howler, a mysterious beast with glowing eyes and a terrifying scream, or the booger dog, a ghostly hound that was said to haunt the woods at night. But most importantly, I learned how to fight back. I learned its weaknesses and strengths and next time I will be ready. Next time I wouldn't be running about like a coward. I would face off against the enemy and I would win.

CHAPTER THREE_
THE MINING CAMP

BACK IN THE seventies I was geology/geophysics student and decided during the summer and before the next term started to take a cross country trip where I was going to meet up with my girlfriend, who was visiting her family in Illinois and drive back with her to college to start the fall semester. She had gone a week earlier to spend the month with her parents and visit some of her old friends and other family because she didn't get to go home much while away at school. I lived only a few towns away from where we went to college and so I got to go home all the time. I was an avid outdoorsman even back then and I was looking forward to it being nothing but me and the open road. I hadn't ever left my home state and hadn't ever traveled very far outside of my hometown even and going to college was the farthest I had ever been in my whole life. I was also planning on checking out some old, abandoned gold mines that were allegedly all over the route to California from where I was living according to some old geological survey map thing that I had found inside of another book in the school's library. It was a risky adventure, that's for sure, because I had no idea and no way of knowing whether the places were still accessible or open for anyone to just go and hang out around either. Also, the only thing I had to work with as far as directions were regular maps and the map that was inside of the book, along with the literature. I blew it up and marked the mines and a few other places that were said to have some rich geological history and set out on my way. I had a beat up old pick-up truck, but I got it serviced before I left and felt confident, I wouldn't have any problems. We didn't have the internet or GPS and we also didn't have cell phones. If the plan failed or if I got stuck somewhere it would have ended up being very bad for me. I was a somewhat poor college student and didn't want to spend all my money on the trip, mainly because I wanted to make some stops at some tourist spots and destinations along the way, on the way back, with my girlfriend.

I was planning on pulling off to the side of the road whenever I got tired and otherwise just setting up camp for a night or two in some of the prospecting areas. They had been abandoned long before I set out to visit them, but I didn't know if there were tours in the areas or not and who or what I would run into. It seemed to me like an adventure, and I really didn't have too much that I was worrying about and tried to stay positive that one of the myriads of things that could have gone very wrong just wouldn't and that I would be okay, and we would both make it back to campus in one piece. My encounter with the invisible entities happened after I had already made it to California. Most of the rest of the trip went well, despite some small hiccups here and there. My girl-friend's parents decided they wanted her to stay an extra week and they had no interest at all in meeting me until I came to pick her up when I would then spend a night or two and we would head back. That should have been a bit of a disappointment to me, but I was excited because California was the place where I knew I would have the most interesting time and the most fun, visiting all the old gold camps. I left out a lot of my plan and the story so that I can focus on the encounter part of it all but just know that I was relieved and knew that I would be able to explore some more and would see her the following week. I decided to hike out to an actual aban-doned mining district out there because I hadn't ever seen such a thing and knew that it would be right up the alley of what I was looking for. I had heard about it when

I stopped along the way to take a shower and grab some food at a rest stop somewhere. I didn't know what I was really expecting but it wasn't what I found.

I basically hiked into a ghost town located in the middle of a forest that stood in the middle of nowhere. There were buildings, many of them, and though all the mines were closed, and the place looked like it had been abandoned a long time ago, it was worth it for me to stay there and explore it just for the history alone. I didn't know who owned it but whoever had wanted to keep people out. I have never seen as many no-trespassing and turn back signs as I did post along the trails and all over this forest. I explored the town a little bit and there wasn't a single other human being there. It looked like no one had been there in a very long time either, not even to do any general upkeep of the property and I could tell that just by the thickness of the dust that sat all over everything. The place was in an extreme state of disrepair. I knew that I had to be careful and as a college student I knew I couldn't afford to be arrested for trespassing or anything and assumed that there was some sort of security there at night. I didn't want to leave just yet though because for one it was starting to get dark outside, and I had hiked for several hours to get there in the first place and secondly because there was still so much, I hadn't seen yet. It somehow and very quickly became about exploring the little mining town and not about the mines or geography anymore. I didn't realize it at the time, but I have often wondered ever since then if I was perhaps somehow being compelled to go into that town and to go back again after the first day. I hiked further uphill and into the woods, behind the mining camp and set up my tent and built a fire. I chose that spot to spend the night because I wanted to be able to see what was happening, if anything, down in the town in the middle of the night. It was only a few buildings, but I have always referred to it as a town and so that's why I keep doing that here too.

I woke up in the middle of the night and noticed there was a light coming from the abandoned town. I got out my binoculars and took a better look and I could see what looked like a shadow move across the window in one of the old buildings where a light was on. I only got to see it for a split second because it seemed like something knew I was watching, and the light went off almost right away. I got goosebumps all over my arms and legs and suddenly felt like something was watching me. I tried my best not to react, but I sat there in that position, on the ground and overlooking the town for a few more minutes. I immediately felt as if something was creeping up behind me. I didn't want to make any sudden movements because I was completely unaware of what types of wildlife were supposed to be in that forest in that area of the country at that time. The goosebumps returned as I felt something breathing down the back of my neck. It was a cool night, and the breath was warm. It only lasted for a second but that's when I decided to turn around. I didn't see anything and was super freaked out and didn't want to go back into my tent just yet. I also didn't want to build a huge fire because I thought that maybe someone was down in the one building in the town and whoever it was would surely see that I was up there. I needed some warmth though and so I lit a very small fire and sat there, just listening, around it. I kept hearing what sounded like a human being slowly walking all around where my little camp was set up. I shined the flashlight out into the woods around me and saw, several times, dark shadows darting back and forth and weaving in and out from behind the trees. I called out and asked who was there, but I didn't get an answer.

It was around three in the morning so I knew I couldn't just hike back down to my truck and get the hell out of there, although that's exactly what I wanted to do. I couldn't take it anymore after about ten minutes though and decided to go and try to confront the person or people who I thought were out there. I thought for sure someone was messing with me and wanted to steal from me or something like that. The fact that it could have been something supernatural or extraterrestrial at play didn't even cross my mind. Not at first anyway. I walked all around and kept seeing the shadows out of the corner of my eye. I left the small fire lit because I didn't plan on being out there for too long. I was hoping to scare whoever it was away from my camp. I suddenly started getting pelted with small rocks and couldn't understand where they were coming from. They seemed to have been coming from up in the trees but every time I looked there was nothing and no one there. I finally shined my flashlight up into one of them and that's when I saw what I was dealing with.

It looked like water. It looked as though water in the shape of a human being got out of a pool or something and just started walking around. It was up in the tree but within a minute or less of shining my light onto it the thing jumped down. I didn't see where it went because it was so dark out there, but I heard it land and could easily see that it wasn't in the tree anymore. I felt a hot breath on the back of my neck again but when I immediately spun around to catch someone there, there was nothing. Then, I saw a dark shadow dart past me again and instantly made the connection between the water looking entity in the tree and the shadow that had just run past me. The shadows I was seeing were the translucent things. I don't pretend to know how it all works but

I was terrified. I remember about a decade later I saw the movie The Predator and immediately started having a panic attack. I knew that the so-called predator entity is exactly what I had seen that night in that strange forest in California. I ended up running back into my tent, turning the flashlight off and praying that whatever those things were didn't kill me or something worse before the sun rose and I could get out of there. Every few minutes I would feel something hit my tent, almost like someone was outside kicking it or pelting it with large rocks, something like that, but I didn't bother to look because I knew I wouldn't see anything. I didn't dare shine the flashlight on them again. Every time I would start to fall asleep the tent would be hit again and when the sun finally came up, I got the hell out of there and never looked back. I would eventually go back to that spot with several of my college buddies and we stayed in one of the buildings in the town, but we didn't see anything strange, and I never mentioned it.

It was only recently when I have been seeing all these random people from all over the world posting on the internet about encounters, they have had with something they're calling the glimmer man entity. Those stories are a little bit different, but they have enough in common with what I encountered that night for me to be satisfied. It's all somehow related. I don't know or want to know what it was I saw or why I was the one to have seen it when I was out there alone. I feel like if they really were as negative as most people say they are then they would have done something to me while I was out there and vulnerable but all they did was keep me awake scaring the hell out of me for a few hours. Then again, I believe in energy vampires and that's probably why they were doing what they were. They were feeding off my fear, plain and simple. I spent the rest of that week in a cheap motel and didn't leave it unless I absolutely had to. I never mentioned it to anyone until recently and the fact that the person I talked about it with didn't question me one little bit, so, I made the decision to send this to you. I don't have any answers, but I think there are a lot of things out there in this big world of ours that we aren't meant to understand as human beings. I also think there's things that human beings aren't supposed to see but for some reason, that night, I was able to get a look at one of them.

CHAPTER FOUR_
BLACK EYED CHILDREN ENCOUNTER

I HAD BEEN WORKING as a custodian for years, taking on the graveyard shift to make ends meet. The solitude of the night had become my companion, and I had grown accustomed to the eerie stillness that enveloped the empty hallways. But little did I know that one fateful night would forever change my perception of the darkness. It was 1999 and a typical quiet evening, with only the hum of the fluorescent lights breaking the silence. As I made my rounds, pushing my cart filled with cleaning supplies, a strange sensation washed over me. A chill ran down my spine, and I couldn't shake the feeling that I was being watched. I went to wash one of the front doors and felt even worse. I pulled my Walkman off my ears and listened to the clear solitude, and I remember chiding myself for such childish behavior. Although, I couldn't help but to feel like

I continued my routine, trying to brush off the unease that gnawed at me. But as I turned a corner, I froze in my tracks. Two figures stood before me at the door, their eyes completely black. Fear gripped me as I stared into their soulless gaze. "Excuse me," one of them said, their voices devoid of any emotion or inflection. "We need to use the restroom." In the back of my mind, I knew that something was off. A feeling that something was wrong with these children. But in my heart, how would I feel if this was one of my children? I would want someone to show kindness.

I hesitated, my mind racing with confusion and terror. These kids had an otherworldly presence about them, and something deep within me screamed to run away. But curiosity got the better of me, and against my better judgment, I opened the door, and I pointed them in the direction of the nearest restroom. There was almost a strange dusty and old smell that followed them. As they walked away, a sense of dread settled over me like a heavy fog. It was almost as if there was a fog that made me feel other worldly. like I wasn't apart of reality. It felt like a gut punch in my stomach. A strange v My heart pounded in my chest as I contemplated what I had just witnessed. Who were those kids? And why did they have those haunting black eyes?

Unable to shake off the encounter, I decided to investigate further. I discreetly followed them down the hallway, keeping a safe distance. They entered the restroom but never came out.in a panic and worry I decided to search the entire school to see where they may have disappeared to but came up empty handed. Confusion overwhelmed me as I cautiously pushed open the door, only to find an empty room, devoid of any sign of those mysterious children. My mind raced with questions and theories, but I knew deep down that I had stumbled upon something inexplicable. The black-eyed kids were not ordinary children; they were something far more sinister. And I had unwittingly crossed paths with them.

From that night on, my perception of the darkness shifted. Every creak and whisper became a potential threat, and the solitude that once brought me comfort now filled me with dread. I couldn't escape the memory of those black eyes, haunting my dreams and infiltrating my waking thoughts. I tried to share my experience with others, but they dismissed it as a figment of my imagination. They couldn't comprehend the terror I had felt in that moment, the primal fear that had consumed me. So, I kept my encounter with the black-eyed kids to myself, silently carrying the burden of that night. But the thing is, they never appeared after that, but I couldn't escape that feeling.

Years have passed since that fateful encounter, but the memory remains etched in my mind. The darkness no longer holds the same allure it once did, for I know now that it conceals secrets far more sinister than we can comprehend. And as a custodian who walks the empty halls of the night, I remain ever vigilant, knowing that the black-eyed kids may lurk in the shadows, waiting for their next unsuspecting victim.

I couldn't shake the feeling that the black-eyed kids were still watching me. Their presence lingered in the back of my mind, a constant reminder of the darkness that lurked just beyond the surface. One night, as I made my rounds through the dimly lit hallways, I noticed a faint whisper echoing through the empty corridors. It was a soft, melodic voice that seemed to beckon me closer. Against my better judgment, I followed the sound, my heart pounding in my chest.

The whispers led me to a forgotten corner of the building, where an old storage room stood. The door creaked open on its rusty hinges, revealing a scene that sent shivers down my spine. The room was filled with drawings and symbols etched onto the walls, all depicting those haunting black eyes. I stepped back in horror, realizing that I had stumbled upon something far more sinister than I could have ever imagined. The black-eyed kids had left their mark, a chilling reminder of their presence within these walls.

Even that couldn't convince me to leave my job. Although I must admit I wear a consecrated cross to give myself a little extra protection. I still work in these halls. I go about my business as if nothing had ever happened. But every time I pass by those doors, I'm reminded of that horrid night. I guess it doesn't help that I feel goosebumps every time I even look at it. I wonder sometimes if they are out there but then again, maybe it's easier for me

CHAPTER FIVE_
DOGMAN ENCOUNTER

I WAS a typical teenage boy in the summer of 2015, looking for ways to make some extra money. My friends and I had heard about this job called corn detasseling, where we could earn a decent paycheck by working in the fields. It seemed like a great opportunity, so we decided to give it a shot.

The work was grueling. The sun beat down on us relentlessly as we trudged through the muddy rows, reaching up to grab the tassels and pull them off. The corn leaves scratched at our skin, leaving behind red marks and tiny cuts. Sweat poured down our faces as we pushed through fatigue, determined to finish each row before moving on to the next. I was just a young boy, growing up in the heartland of Iowa. The summer of 2015 was hotter than usual. Never underestimate the humidity that corn gives off I can tell you with 100 percent certain. So, this particular summer, I found myself needing extra money for a new bike or even a car. It was hard work, but it paid well, and I was determined to save up for something special.

One particular day stands out vividly in my memory. It started like any other, with our crew gathering at the crack of dawn to begin our work. We split into teams and headed out to our designated sections of the field. I was paired up with my friend Jake, and together we set off into the sea of corn.

As we made our way through the rows, we couldn't shake the feeling that something was off. The usual sounds of birds chirping, and insects buzzing were eerily absent. The air felt heavy, as if a storm was brewing just beyond the horizon. But we dismissed our unease as mere imagination and continued on. You hear all sorts of strange things in the fields. I once saw a deer making a barking noise. I remember laughing with Jake because we both got spooked by it. I was so grateful for having him there. It made the heat filled days easier to do. We usually work side by side.

Hours passed, and the sun climbed higher in the sky. We were nearing the end of our section when we heard a rustling sound coming from behind us. We turned to see a figure emerging from the cornstalks. It was tall and hunched over, with matted fur covering its body. A growl escaped its throat, and I froze unable to believe what I was seeing ahead of me. Thick muscles tissue rippled beneath the fur as it made eye contact with me. There was a gold flickering in his eyes that almost looked like double pupils. I hit Jake's arm, unable to speak. He looked over at me saying, "what?" I pointed at the Dogman. He froze alongside me.

My heart skipped a beat as I realized what we were facing: the legendary Dogman. Stories of this creature had circulated among locals for years, but I had always dismissed them as mere them as crazy talk. There would have been some sort of evidence if something like this ever existed. Yet here it stood before us, its glowing red eyes fixed on our trembling forms.

Jake and I froze in fear, unable to tear our gaze away from the menacing creature. Its growls reverberated through the air, sending chills down our spines. We knew we had to get away, but our legs felt like jelly, refusing to obey our frantic commands. The dog man crotched lower limbs working like a cat ready to hunt. Suddenly, the Dogman lunged towards us, its claws slashing through the air. Adrenaline surged through my veins as I found the strength to move. I grabbed Jake's arm, and we sprinted through the cornfield, desperate to escape the clutches of this terrifying beast.

We ran as fast as our legs could carry us, the sound of our pounding footsteps echoing in our ears. The cornstalks whipped against our faces, leaving scratches and welts in their wake. But we didn't dare look back, fearing that even a momentary glance would seal our fate. Finally, we burst out of the cornfield and stumbled onto a nearby road. We collapsed onto the ground, gasping for breath, and thanking whatever higher power had spared us from the Dogman's wrath. We knew we had narrowly escaped a gruesome fate.

From that day forward, I never looked at the cornfields of Iowa in the same way. The encounter with the Dogman had forever changed me, leaving me with a lingering sense of unease whenever.

CHAPTER SIX_
THE FAIRY LIGHTS

I RECENTLY STARTED SEEING people all over the internet talking about the fae or fairies, and how they have had interactions with them throughout their lives and it rang a bell for me. After I had gone through many stories a day for several weeks it suddenly dawned on me that a long time ago, I had an encounter with what I have always believed was the fae folk, when I was camping in New Mexico as a young girl. I was with my father, my mother and two of my older siblings. We used to go camping all the time and my siblings and I really didn't have much else to do with our free time as children than to play in the woods that surrounded our home. The encounter takes place when we went on a trip for a weekend to celebrate my father's birthday. There's nothing my old man loved more than being in the great outdoors and he really made sure to go out of his way to instill that same love in his children. We were all excited for the trip even though we had to drive, altogether in the car, for about eight hours to get to the spot we would normally go to. My mother had made reservations months in advance and while we were visiting a proper campsite, just like everyone else's family at the time, we had our own secret spots where there were little or no other people around. We wanted to spend as much time as we could without too many people being around. My parents were both very introverted and that's a trait they passed on to me and several of my siblings too. My grandparents were Irish immigrants and "straight off the boat" as people said in my day. They came to the United States without any money and not knowing even a word of the language. I bring that up so you understand that I grew up hearing stories from them about the fairies and the magical lands from which they would come and visit us humans, here on our own third dimensional plane. It always fascinated me and my siblings and even when they all got too old for those stories and somewhat outgrew them, I was never able to shake the feeling that maybe there was something to the stories after all. I have no idea if my belief in them is what made them choose me that night so long ago, but I like to think that's what it was, and I have had many other encounters with them throughout the years. That was the first one and that's why it's so special. Also, I wasn't the only one who saw them that night and it made it impossible for anyone else in my family who was there to ignore the fact that maybe my grandparents knew what they had been talking about after all.

We arrived at the campgrounds at around two in the afternoon and that gave us plenty of time to hike to one of my father's secret spots, as he liked to call them. My siblings and I were so excited we could barely contain ourselves. Spending all that time smushed into the back seat of the car had really gotten to us and we all couldn't wait to stretch our legs and move around. We left our parents to set things up and mom started dinner around four or five while we all played in the woods. There was a lake somewhere on site, but we weren't planning on visiting it until the following day anyway, so we were left to entertain ourselves just as we normally did at home. I was around ten years old at the time and I eventually wandered a bit further than my siblings wanted to venture and that's also something that was very common back then. It started that afternoon, when I heard random humming coming from somewhere out there in the woods with me. I thought that I was alone but after following the humming sounds and not seeing anyone nearby for a good fifteen minutes, it dawned on me that one of my sisters was playing a prank on me or something. I don't know what I was thinking though because the humming was frightening in any way and in fact, I feel now like I was literally being entranced to follow the lovely tune. It was working. I thought too that maybe there was a woman or another female child somewhere around that could have been the source of the beautiful song but again, I didn't see anyone for a long while.

Eventually I came to a very large tree that looked like it didn't belong in that forest or, at the very least, that it didn't belong where it was, among the other trees in that area. It was beautiful and looked like it hadn't spent a day in any inclement weather despite it being larger than all the others. I knew it had to have been there for a very long time just based on the sheer size of it. I was a bit put off and confused when I realized the sound of the humming was coming from the tree, but I still confidently walked up to it and looked inside of the medium sized hole that was right there on the front of it. Before I could see what was in there, I heard my sister's voice behind me asking what I was doing. She startled me and I jumped a little before turning to face her. I told her I was trying to figure out where the humming had been coming from, but she just looked at me like I was crazy and said that she hadn't heard any humming. She told me that dinner was ready and that confused me as well because I thought I had only been gone for a half hour, tops, and yet it had been over an hour since I had separated from my siblings. I shrugged and walked away from the beautiful tree with my sister. I didn't hear any humming on the walk back or again at all that day. I soon forgot all about the whole situation and eventually it was time for bed. Since we would camp a lot, even sometimes spending nights outside in the woods by our house when we were bored or desperate to do something as a family on short notice, we had some pretty good equipment. That included several very large tents. They would sleep three adults, but we set it up where my sister and I would sleep in one, my parents in another and my other two siblings that had come on the trip with us in the third one. We had plenty of room and everyone was more than comfortable. I remember falling asleep very quickly and almost immediately dreaming of that strange and somewhat out of place tree. I awoke with a start in the middle of the night. The moon outside was shining bright enough that it wasn't pitch black outside, despite the vast amount of tree coverage in that area. I rubbed my eyes and was just about to get up and use the bathroom when I saw something very strange.

It looked like little twinkling lights floating all

around outside of the tent. It was incredibly bright, and I woke my sister up right away so that she could see it too. She was amazed but neither one of us was feeling brave enough to get out of the tent and see what the heck was happening. It looked like the stars were just incredibly close at first, until they all started moving. The lights were teeny tiny, smaller than my child's pinky fingernail was at the time and there had to have been hundreds of them just floating all around out there. Though the tent wasn't clear, I could see all the colors dancing around very clearly. I whispered to my sister and asked her what she thought it could be and she said it was obvious to her that it was the fae folk our grandparents had told us about so many times. There were all different colors and some of them I don't even know the proper name for. I think whatever dimension the fairies come from has different colors, more colors, than we do here on earth. We watched for about a minute, until we both started to hear what sounded like little children giggling and a woman humming. It was too much then and I needed to see what was happening with my own eyes and without the tent between me and whatever it was. I asked my sister to come out with me and though at first, she refused, she eventually relented. She was just as curious as I was, I guess. We got out of our tent and just stood there. The humming sounded like it was coming from farther off in the woods, but the giggling was coming from the tiny creatures that were fluttering all around us. They really did look like stars that had somehow fallen from the sky. Within a minute or two of watching the spectacular light show our other two siblings had stepped out of their tent as well and the four of us were just standing there in awe, watching what was happening before us with disbelief in our eyes.

None of us moved but suddenly the humming turned into an evil sounding cackle, and we all started to look around. The lights of the little pixies, that's what I assumed they were then, and I still think that to this day, dimmed and then went out one by one. It was dark, except for the light of the moon and the actual stars. We could no longer see the fairies, but we all knew that they were there. The energy had shifted completely, and we felt like we were in some sort of danger. We all wanted to wake our parents up but none of us could move. A shadowy figure came walking out of the woods as the sound of the humming got closer and closer. We never saw what the source was, not completely anyway, but we did see what looked like a black hood and blazing red eyes peeking out at us from behind a tree. It came from around the tree after a minute, but it still looked like nothing more than a solid shadow with red eyes. Suddenly I heard my siblings yelling "ouch" and making other sounds that told me they were being hurt or some-thing. I suddenly felt like I was being stung, repeatedly and all over my body, by hornets. I knew what that felt like because I had been stung many times in my short life at that point. We were all running around and flailing our arms like crazy, trying to shake off whatever was stinging us. After a few moments of that our parents got out of their tent and demanded to know what was happening. Just like that, the stinging, humming, and giggling had stopped and there seemed to be no more danger around us. We were all crying as we tried to explain to our parents what had just happened to us. Of course, they didn't believe us, and we were terrified to stay at that camp for the whole night, in the dark and by ourselves in the tents. They shined a flashlight on our bodies and saw welts that were swollen and unlike anything they had ever seen before. Our parents were concerned that there was some sort of dangerous and possibly deadly poisonous insect out there and so we left at the first sign of light that morning.

We didn't have the kind of money my parents would have needed to take four kids to the doctor and so we just put a salve on the wounds and eventually they healed. Our other siblings didn't believe us either when we told them but of course our grandparents did. They said that from that point on we would have to bring offerings of respect into any woods we entered with us for as long as we lived to not become a target of the fairies' wrath again. We always brought extra sweets or honey with us whether we were going camping or just playing in the woods by our house. Our parents, who at their age were sick of the fairy stories, always rolled their eyes, as did our siblings who hadn't been there that night. While I have had many more encounters with the fairies since that night, they've not ever been as unpleasant as that first time and I think that is because I still to this day will bring some sweets or alcohol with me into the woods, no matter the reason why I am in them in the first place. I was put off from camping for a little while but when you are so young you don't have a choice sometimes but to go where your parents want you to go and so it didn't make much of a difference to them. I think that perhaps I had angered them when I put my head into the hole in the tree, which by the way reminds me I still cannot remember a moment of that lost time that I had when I did that. I've been looking lately for more answers because my parents and grandparents are now deceased and I have found a plethora of information on the internet, most of it is garbage but some of it makes sense and seems legitimate. I just wanted to add to the latter kind with this story of my own. Thanks for letting me share it and helping to get the real information out there. The fairies do not like humans, period, and we should always be careful not to anger them or draw attention to ourselves at all whiles out in the woods. It is after all their home, not ours, and we are only guests out there.

CHAPTER SEVEN_
A TERRIFYING GLITCH IN THE MATRIX

THIS IS something that happened to me when I was a little boy and I lived in a tiny village in some mountains in the United States. It was a strange way to grow up, by today's standards, but the community I grew up in, in that village, was very tight knit and it wasn't often that anyone ever left it to go anywhere else. Everything we needed was at our disposal there and the adults and kids alike all worked equally as hard to keep it all running properly so that we didn't have to depend on outside sources for things like food and clothing. My encounter happened one day when I was with a group of other boys my age, we were no older than eight at the time, and we were with some of the other men in the village gathering sticks and wood for one purpose or another. My mother woke me up and my siblings and I had breakfast before each of us got dressed and were given our assigned duties for that day. I was on wood gathering duty which was one of the easier tasks and so I was somewhat elated. I was running a little bit behind and by the time I made it out my front door, everyone else that was going with me that day was already waiting for me there. They all seemed annoyed but didn't show it and we went on about our way silently, for the most part. We were all friends but when it was time to work, we didn't talk much because it was frowned upon by the elders in the village. The country was going through a great depression at the time and if we somehow messed up the jobs we were given on any given day, people could freeze or starve to death. It was a lot to have to deal with as such a young kid, but I didn't know that at the time and thought everyone lived that way.

We broke off into groups of three as we entered the woods and were told when to return to the meeting place, which was right where we were all grouping together. The forest was dense and vast, but we knew the perimeter we were to stay inside of. We were taught from a very young age the places where we were to gather one thing or another from and where we shouldn't have been going unsupervised. Once the grown-ups left us to go about their own business, we of course started joking and having some fun with our tasks while still making sure to put in great effort towards the task at hand. We were finally done and ready to meet back up with the rest of the group and the grown-ups for lunch. We picked up our baskets and carried them but it's like we couldn't find our way out of the area and back to where we had originally started from. It was an easy trail that we had all taken hundreds of times before, but it seemed like no matter what we did we just couldn't make our way out. We didn't see anything that looked unfamiliar or anything like that, but we somehow kept ending up in a circle. This went on for hours and eventually we could hear a bunch of men from the village calling all our names. They sounded tired, scared and a bit desperate but even as we called back to them, they never seemed to hear us. We never saw them either, despite it seeming like they were very close to where we were wandering around. Eventually the sun started to set, and we started to really panic.

One of the boys in the group started to cry and then he started to pray which led myself and the third boy to join him in those prayers. Within minutes we saw the trail we had been looking for and though we knew something was very wrong with the whole situation, we were just glad to have been getting out of there. Little did we know it was only the beginning of our ordeal. We had taken that trail into the area where we had been collecting the wood and we all knew it well, as I've already stated. We could still hear the men calling for us and we kept calling back but once we started walking the trail towards where it originally seemed like their voices were calling from and towards where we were supposed to have met the rest of the group in the first place, we could no longer hear them and just decided to walk back to our homes. We were exhausted and scared, and we didn't want to be alone in the woods at night for too long. It appears the men who had been sent to find and rescue us weren't hearing us for one reason or another and so we thought that it would just be easier on us to go home. Within two minutes of walking on that very familiar trail, we noticed something was very different about it. It seemed like it was much longer. Usually if we walked about ten minutes in one direction, we would reach the original spot where we always broke off and went about the task of gathering wood. However, we couldn't see any of the usual landmarks and it just looked like the forest kept on going and going. We were absolutely terrified at that point and didn't know what to do next. We decided to keep walking because we knew that no matter what, eventually we would come to some-one's home, even if it wasn't one of our own, and they could help us get to our homes and reunite with our respective families. That didn't seem to be working either and once again it was like we were just in some sort of endless loop on the trail just like we had been earlier in the night while we had been looking for it in the first place.

One moment we would all recognize a funny looking tree or a bush or something else but then the very next moment it would all look the same and be completely unfamiliar. Not only didn't we hear the men calling for us anymore, but we didn't hear anything at all. It was pitch dark outside and we had been walking for what seemed like the entire night. We had taken a break to go and try to have lunch at noon and it was already very dark. Though we all had watches on our wrists, they had all stopped at a different time, within moments of one another, earlier in the day. They had all stopped right after we stopped to take our lunch break. We were starving, terrified and very confused and none of us wanted anything more than to be at home with our families. We started wondering if we would die out there. It was about an hour of walking that trail before we got to the tunnel that led back into the village. It should've taken no more than twenty minutes and that's if we were really moving slowly. The tunnel was eventually within our sight, so we were relieved and tried not to think about getting stuck in an endless loop of wandering down there too, as we had when we tried to find and get off the trail. We entered the tunnels and there was very little light. None of us had ever been in it before when it was dark outside and luckily, we had all been trained to survive out in the wilderness should something like this ever happen. Well, not anything exactly like what was happening to us but something like us getting lost or what have you. We all had small flashlights on us, and we turned them on. That's when we started to hear a strange noise coming from behind us. Of course, when we turned to look, there was nothing there. I should mention here that the tunnel was a series of them, all underground, that led back to our little village which was itself located in the middle of nowhere. There was some water in them, but it was only ankle deep in the area where we were walking. We knew that it could have been deeper in other parts of the tunnel, but we hadn't ever been in any of those parts as the children of the village weren't allowed to wander into them. We almost never went anywhere without an adult accompanying us and I've often wondered if they knew something more than what they had always let on, but I was never answered when I asked so I don't know. I think they did though.

Whatever it was, it sounded like something was wading through water that was at least knee deep and though we wanted to lie to one another and to ourselves and say that it had to have been one of the adults who were sent out to look for us, we all knew better. We didn't call out to whoever it was and in fact we became as silent as we possibly could. Still, it sounded like whatever it was, it was following us closely. It made no sense I know because as I said already, when we turned around and shined the lights behind us there was nothing there. The only thing in the tunnel was the tunnel, meaning there was nowhere for anyone to hide or anything like that. It was very eerie, and we were all silently bawling at that point. We knew we were in the presence of absolute evil, but we had no idea why we felt that way at all. We just knew it as an absolute fact. Whatever it was sounded somehow too like it was trying very hard to be quiet and may not have realized that the sound of the splashing water under its feet each time it took a step was giving it away. Eventually we couldn't take anymore and started to run. We emerged from the tunnel into one more patch of woods we had to walk for a very short time to make it to a house. We knew everyone in the tiny little village and so it didn't matter to whose house we ended up because they would surely have known that we were all missing, and the man of the house would either take us home or we would wait for him, and he would take us once he got back. He would have been nowhere except searching for us because no one went out at night into the woods for any reason.

We all stopped for a moment to catch our breaths and heard the splashing water under the foot of whatever had been following us all along down there. We all ran and hid as best as we could behind some nearby trees. We had abandoned our collected wood in the tunnel right when we heard someone behind us, stalking us, because we knew eventually, we might have had to make a run for it. The very dim lights inside of the tunnel helped us to see the shape of whatever it was, and it was horrific looking to say the very least. The eyes glowed bright yellow and looked like that of some sort of reptilian creature. It looked around and the skin on it looked very rough and like most of it was scaly with things sticking out of it all over the place. It growled and sounded angry. We couldn't see much of it at first until it took a few steps towards us. That's when we saw it in its full glory. It was around eight feet tall and honestly looked just like a giant lizard. It walked on two legs, and it looked like there was water dripping off its entire body. It must have been swimming as well as walking for it to have been as wet as it was and emerging from where we did. I say that because the water was only ankle deep for at least a mile from where we entered to where we exited, and it had been following us almost the whole time. I didn't understand how we hadn't been able to see it when we would turn and shine the lights on it, not at first anyway. It breathed very heavily and looked all around but it seemed like it jumped and was shocked or something when the voices of the men came booming through the woods again as they called our names out loud. We all screamed, and the creature bent down as though it were going to crawl on all fours back into the tunnel. However, it got on all fours and took about two steps that way before slowly phasing out altogether. We watched in horror as we all came out from behind the trees we were hiding behind and we saw the water still moving as if something was there. Well, something was there, and we knew what it was but just couldn't see it anymore. We screamed again.

It took them five minutes to find us, and we were all brought back to our homes. We tried repeatedly to explain what had happened to us. We explained about the barrier that seemed to be stopping us from getting onto the trail and how the trail went on for miles and miles. We even told them all about the creature, but we were in a lot of trouble and told that we weren't going to make the village suffer for our nonsense. We were put on extra hard work duty for an entire month, seven days a week, effective the very next day. We weren't allowed out of the sight of at least one adult for months after that but honestly that's probably what saved our lives. I think we accidentally stumbled on some sort of portal that's directly parallel with our world and that perhaps intermingles with our world from time to time. I never saw the creature again and I lived in that village until I was twenty years old. I still have a very hard time going into the woods and have been living in a big city with a very high population ever since that time. I know what I saw now when I think about it, and I knew then. Whatever that thing was, I thoroughly believe it's why kids weren't allowed in the woods alone at night, why we had a curfew and why even the grown-ups didn't leave their homes after dark. The village no longer exists, at least not how it did in the thirties and now the forest has been cleared around it and the tunnels closed. It's a bigger town now and I don't even know if the people who live there are aware of the history of their little town which is why I didn't mention it specifically by name. I lost contact with those boys long ago, but I remember they didn't ever want to discuss it and in fact acted like I was a crazy person whenever I would try and bring it up so eventually, I just stopped doing so altogether. That's my one and only paranormal encounter although, it could just as easily have been extraterrestrial in nature, as far as I know about it all now. Thanks for letting me get it all down on paper before I can't remember it anymore.

CHAPTER EIGHT_

BIGFOOT ENCOUNTER AT A CONSTRUCTION
SITE

BACK IN 2007, I was sent to Texas as a group of
reinforcements from my construction company in Florida. We were asked to assist with a building construction
project that my company was doing. This was a major
project for us, and we were behind on schedule. To
compensate and in hopes of catching up, since all the
work and wiring was being done on the interior, we went
to a 24/7 rotating shift, seven days a week. Being the
newest electrician to join the crew, I ended up getting
the graveyard shift.

The area where the building was going up was very
wooded, in the Piney Woods of East Texas, and on the
outskirts of town which allowed for more expansion and
the inevitable growth of the town. The outside lighting
of the complex was limited to basic security lighting

since the building was still under construction. The exterior of the building was complete, and the front of the building was all glass windows. All the work we were doing involved the build out on the inside, so the building was lit up brightly. So, while there were no "exterior" lights, the area was brightly lit up from the interior rooms and lit the surrounding complex and extended out to the guard shack. The complex was surrounded by a ten-foot-tall fence with barbed wire to make sure no one or no animals were entering the property.

One night, during a break outside, I found myself in an open area surrounded by the densest woods I've ever seen. The woods were thick on the east side of the complex and we only had security lights around the perimeter of the building, but there was a full moon out that night. I was walking around, stretching my legs, and warming up before going back inside. Over on the other side of the fence, something caught my attention. I saw it out of the corner of my eye. There was a figure that was moving in the woods. It seemed to step out from behind a tree and walk around, like it was looking for something. It kicked branches and moved rocks and leaves with its foot. I didn't know if it was searching or foraging for something to eat. It never looked over in my direction and it acted like it could care less if I was there.

I watched for about 30 seconds, wondering what would be out in the woods at 3 a.m. The complex backed up to a nature preserve, so it could be almost anything. I watched as it vanished deeper into the woods, and I was unable to discern any distinct details, except that it stood upright, was bipedal, covered in dark hair, and notably taller than me. I am a bit over six feet tall and this creature was about a foot taller than I am. I was curious and perplexed at what I saw shifting around the trees.

I didn't say anything to anyone when I got back to work, but after a few nights, it was really bothering me, so I discreetly asked my co-workers a few days later if they ever saw anything in the woods at night. Not surprisingly, none of them had ever witnessed anything like it in the area.

Over the next few days, I started noticing that people were snickering and laughing when I walked by, so I assumed my story of the big hairy creature in the woods had gotten around the building. I decided to not mention it again to anyone and just concentrate on my job. I made sure that if I took a break outside again, I took it on the other side of the complex. I didn't want to take a chance outside alone in the middle of the night. Since I didn't get a good look at what was out there, I wasn't going to press my luck and end up in some sort of crazed Texas Skirmish alone in the middle of the Piney

Woods. All I knew is whatever was out there that night was big, much bigger than I was.

Initially, I considered the possibility that it might have been a black bear roaming around. However, black bears aren't known to inhabit this region of Texas. It would have been highly unlikely for one to have migrated from Louisiana just to pay us a visit and I really don't think a black bear could have walked on two legs if this creature did.

A few days after my conversation with a few of my co-workers, one of the security guards - an ex-Marine - told me he contacted the local Sheriff's department about a month earlier. He said he had a sighting in the same vicinity during one of his night shift perimeter checks and since this was a multi-million-dollar project, anyone near the building that late at night was probably up to no good. The security guard leaned in a bit closer and confided in me that we were in "Bigfoot Country" as he called it. The guard said he had been patrolling and heard loud knockings on the trees out in the woods. He said it sounded like large branches being hit against the trunk of a tree and it had a definite rhythm to it. He seemed to be up on his Bigfoot lore and started to tell me more about the smells and how the creatures disappeared so quickly into the dark forest when he got nearby. I hadn't given it much thought, but to hear him talk about the things he had seen at night while on patrol made me start to believe that the large figure, I saw in the woods was a lone Bigfoot, looking for food. I would never admit it to anyone, but he really started to have me doubt myself and to consider it was a Bigfoot that I saw in the woods. The security guard reporting this incident further added weight to the strange phenomenon and events that were occurring in the area.

CHAPTER NINE_
BEASTS OF ITALY

My GRANDPARENTS WERE BORN and raised in Italy and came over here when my father was three years old. They eventually moved back there, and my family and I would go visit them every year during the summer. They lived in a simple little village with even less to do than in my hometown in Arkansas. There were a lot of woods, and everyone grew what they ate and made their own clothes. It was a financially poor community, but it was filled with happiness, and everyone seemed to get along well. The whole village was like one big family and from the first time I ever visited there, from what I was told and from what I experienced when I got older, I was considered to be one of their own. I loved the woods that surrounded the village the most and I would go and play in them for hours with other boys my age. We always got along, and those boys became like brothers to me. One year when I went to visit the vibe felt off from the very beginning. I remember the adults all whispering and talking in hushed tones. People weren't out in the streets or sitting on their front stoops like they always had been every other year I had gone to visit. It was warm outside and so I thought that I would be spending the summer playing with the other boys like I always had but when I would go and ask at their homes if they could come out, their mothers would smile down at me and tell me that they weren't available to see me at that time and to try again another day. This went on for an entire month until finally I asked my parents what happened and if I had inadvertently done something to offend the other kids or their parents. I was fourteen years old at the time and had grown up hanging out with those boys every single summer, every single day, and all day long. I was hurt at first and thought I had done something I wasn't aware of. There had always been a language barrier, but we always managed to communicate just fine. I had even picked up a good amount of Italian throughout the years though at that time I still couldn't speak it fluently. Finally, my father sat me down to talk to me about it but all he would say is, "this is a very superstitious town and right now no one wants to leave their homes." He smiled at me as he said it but no matter how many questions, I asked he wouldn't give me any answers or any more information. It was very frustrating and for the first time I felt like an outsider in my beloved Italian village.

My grandparents were adamant that I stay inside but I didn't want to spend the entire summer alone in the house with my family and I was itching to get out into the woods to do some fishing. Finally, after a week or so of begging them, my parents relented. I remember listening to my father argue with my grandfather in Italian and it sounded like the conversation was very heated. My father handed me my fishing gear and told me which spot was best to go and fish in. I hadn't ever been in the woods or fishing alone there, but I figured it would be just like home and no problem. I was excited because I had been all cooped up inside ever since we had gotten there, and I loved to be out in mother nature. I also wanted to catch some fish for dinner as a sort of peace offering to my grandparents. They seemed angrier with my mom and dad than with me, but I knew they were upset and would've preferred it if I hadn't gone out that day. It seemed like they didn't want me to go out at all and I just didn't understand it. How could I have understood when no one would tell me anything? I walked through the village and into the woods and I felt something was strange about it right away. However, I was not raised to be superstitious or paranoid and so I brushed it off as my being weirded out my first time alone in those creepy and vast, very dense woods. They were very intimidating to me as a child and being there alone was a whole new experience than when I would go with ten or fifteen other boys my age. I was determined though, if nothing else, and after about twenty minutes I made it to the spot where my father had suggested I go and try my luck. I sat on a giant rock and set everything up. I could see the fish in the water at first and knew that I was going to have a great catch that day. Well, that's what I thought that I knew, anyway.

I forgot to mention that by the time I talked my way out of the house I only had about two hours until dusk. One thing my parents were adamant about was that I be home before it got dark and not a second after. I knew my parents weren't ever strict with me so when they put their foot down like that I listened. I had every intention of being home, with a ton of fresh fish, by the time dusk settled down on the village. The road to hell is paved with good intentions, so they say. It started off normal enough and I caught three large fish in my first half hour of being out there. Suddenly though it seemed like all the fish had been scared away by something. I watched as they started swimming in circles and banging into one another. It was bizarre behavior, at least as far as what I knew about that particular type of fish and fish in general and I had never seen fish behave that way before. I watched in wonder and awe but there was some fear deep down inside of me as well. As I stood there, confused, and watching all the fish swim away, I noticed the ground below me was vibrating. I looked around but there was absolutely nothing in sight that could have been making that happen to the ground. I figured the fish sensed something that I didn't and was thinking about just packing up and leaving right then. I wish I had done that sometimes. Other times, I'm kind of glad I stayed. I realized suddenly too that there were no animals around on the land or in the trees around me and that everything had gone eerily silent. I had seen some horror movies before, though I didn't really care for them and found them very foolish most of the time. I swear at that moment I felt something bad was coming. I immediately started thinking it was somehow supernatural, whatever was happening with the animals and the fish, and my fears were confirmed when I threw a rock into the water. There was no splash. I mean, the splash was there but it made no sound at all. The water splashed onto my arm as I looked around again. I heard loud howling sounds, and they were coming from more than one place inside of those woods. Whatever was coming for me, there was more than one of them.

My mind was screaming for me to turn and run,

even insisting I leave my catch and all my gear behind, but my body wasn't moving. I just stood there, and it seemed like everything was happening in slow motion. I didn't drink or do drugs so I knew I couldn't have been hallucinating. I saw the trees shaking and realized it was almost dusk. It sounded like a stampede of some kind of large animal was coming right at me and I finally just took off and started running. I ran as fast as my legs could carry me and left everything behind. I heard a crashing sound and thought how angry my father would be that I left my fishing gear and pole behind because I had a weird feeling about something, so I made the mistake of turning around and going back to grab it all. I walked slowly back to where my stuff was because heard strange groaning and grunting noises coming from that exact spot. I also heard what sounded like someone banging pots or something. I hid behind a tree and that's when I saw three giant creatures. They were all huddled over my belongings, but had they been standing upright they would have been at least eleven feet tall. They were incredibly wide as well and covered in dark brown hair that was long and all over their bodies. I tried not to scream as I watched them rip my cooler apart with their bare hands and fight over the fish inside. They pushed one another and grunted. They howled loudly and pounded on their chests. One of them came from behind and knocked the other two to the ground, grabbing all three fish in one foul swoop and taking off again into the woods. It sounded like a monkey, but it also sounded like it was laughing at or mocking the two it had just knocked over. It took them a moment to get up and once they did, one of them noticed me and started howling and screaming, pointing in my direction to alert the other one to my presence. They both just stood there and stared at me for a good minute or more and then they made a sniffing noise, as if they were completely disgusted by my presence and wanted nothing to do with me. They turned and ran off after the one that had just taken the fish I had so diligently waited for and caught. I was stunned and more confused than anything else. I walked quickly back into the village.

I didn't run. I wasn't fearful of the creatures I just saw, somehow. I had been more terrified when it was something unknown and that I couldn't see that I had heard and felt was coming for me. I was more scared at that moment of telling my parents and grandparents what had just happened, why I was home after dark and what had happened to my gear and fishing pole. Not to mention my cooler, which was my grandfathers. I got into the house, and they were all just sitting there at the kitchen table waiting for me. They all turned and stared, and it reminded me somewhat like the creatures I had seen in the woods, when they had stopped what they were doing and turned to face me. I tried to explain but before I got even two words out my grandfather had his belt out and my grandmother was crying into her hands. My parents calmed them down and invited me to sit with them and tell them what happened. I thought for sure they wouldn't believe me, but they all just sat there, staring at me with their mouths hanging open, like they were stunned or something. There was an awkward five minutes where it dawned on me why the creatures in the woods didn't scare me despite being possibly supernatural and gigantic. I realized their eyes had been human. They looked at me like my family was looking at me just then and that's when I put it together. I was sent to bed without supper and made to spend the rest of the summer in the sights of either one of my parents or grandparents. A part of me wanted to go back into the woods and see the creatures again and the other part of me wanted nothing to do with them and kept having nightmares of them chasing me down and tearing me apart like they had done to my grandfather's cooler. No one ever explained anything to me, but I did notice my father and grandfather, along with a lot of other men in the town all getting together once it got dark outside and going into the woods with guns. I never bothered asking questions because I knew I wouldn't get an answer anyway.

It didn't dawn on me that I had witnessed three bigfoot until much later in my life. I tried to talk to my family about it but none of them wanted to hear it. In fact, every time I would bring up my experience, they would all just start incessantly crossing themselves as though I had said or done something bad or evil. I never saw them again even though I did go into those woods around the village many times after that and still do to this day when I visit my parents who also retired to Italy. They live in my grandparent's old house which they inherited once my grandparents passed in the late nineties. I don't know what it all means but I hope to see one again now that I am an adult and much more educated about the phenomenon. I always wondered if they speak telepathically like some people say that they do and what they might've said to me that day so long ago if anything at all. What would one say to me now? I have no idea, no way of knowing and because I haven't been able to find one, I wonder if I will ever get the answers that I've been looking for. Thanks for letting me share.

CHAPTER TEN_
FOLLOWED BY EVIL

IT's no secret that a lot of people like to retreat into the woods to escape the rigors of everyday life and reality in general. It's peaceful out there in the middle of mother nature and up until I was about fifteen years old, I felt the same way about it. However, once I had the experience I did while out camping with my best friend back in 1973, I have never been the same again. I also haven't ever gone into the woods again, for the most part, at night or even when it was dusk. Whatever we saw out there stayed with us and it's something that, though I've never physically seen it again, it has haunted my nightmares in all the years since. My best friend back then is still my best friend today and she and I share that evil experience and she feels the same way as I do about it. She also has nightmares and has avoided the woods at night at all costs ever since. No one believed us back then but for the most part, when we tell the story nowadays, people seem to at least give us the benefit of the doubt. We didn't do drugs or drink at all and in fact we weren't popular with most of the other kids in our school at the time because of our "goody goody" ways. That was neither here nor there for us and we enjoyed each other's company, as we still do. Here is the story of what happened to us and what could happen to you if you aren't careful and find yourself messing around with things you couldn't possibly understand.

Our families were friends as well so a lot of the time we would all vacation together. My best friend, Emily, had an older brother who was the same age as my own older brother, and she had one younger sister. Our mothers and fathers had all gone to high school together, the same high school we attended, in the same small town. We even had some of the same teachers as they did. I know that's wild when you really think about it, but it wasn't that uncommon back in those days. We grew up in rural Kentucky surrounded by roads that seemed to go on for miles and miles and lead to nowhere. Emily and I would spend hours walking along those roads and hanging out in the woods that surrounded them. There wouldn't be a house in sight, no signs of normal civilization and we could go hours without seeing or hearing another human being. She and I always had interests that other people considered bizarre and that our very religious parents were horrified by. We thought it was all in good fun, as we learned new ways to try and divine our futures and connect with the spirit world. We knew our parents had an end of the school year camping trip planned for all of us and we decided it was a good idea to sneak a Ouija board in with our stuff. The way we ended up with that board is another story altogether, but it isn't too relevant to the encounter we ended up having so I will just say we stole it from a shop near our home. The owner of the shop was said to be a devil worshiper and a witch, but not a good one. She was a mean old woman who seemed to hate kids our age and getting it out of the store was a mission in and of itself. However, I often wonder now if the old hag knew all along what we were doing and what we had done, and if it was her doing, what happened to us.

We all set off in a campervan, but we weren't going to all be staying in it together. It was big enough for the twelve-hour drive and seven people, but it wouldn't sleep all of us. Me and Emily and both of our brothers would sleep outside with our parents and her baby sister inside. It was the first year the adults would be sleeping inside and allowing us kids to sleep on the outside and we were excited. Our older brothers were typical for that time, and they mocked and picked on us relentlessly so she and I had a plan that we thought would work and allow us the time, space, and privacy we needed to use the pilfered board. Eventually we got to the campsite and spent the whole night hanging out by the fire, eating, and having a great time with our families. Eventually though it was time to go to sleep and that's when Emily and I enacted our plan. We picked a fight with our brothers and then begged our parents to let us go further into the woods, just a little bit, so we could have some privacy overnight. They eventually relented because they knew our brothers would be right there within ear shot. Also, they knew no matter how much we fought they wouldn't let anything happen to us should they hear us screaming or otherwise in some distress. I could tell our moms were nervous, but they let us go and Emily and I walked for about five minutes deeper into the woods. We only needed it to be far enough away that the boys wouldn't hear our whispers or notice the tealight candles we planned on lighting during our Ouija board session.

Emily and I had some whispered conversations about how to use the board. We had recently watched a horror movie that had a Ouija board in it, and everyone died at the end except one person. You would think that would have deterred us from ever even going near one, but you would be wrong, and it only made us want to try one even more. Back in the early seventies, where we come from, it was considered evil and demonic to want to speak with the dead, but Emily and I were just planning on asking it basic and somewhat silly questions about boys we liked and teachers we didn't like, stuff like that. We weren't taking it seriously at all and that was our first, worst and biggest mistake. As soon as we no longer heard our brothers, we took the board and the candles out. We were both sitting on our sleeping bags across from one another and we had the board in the middle. The only candles we had were four little, half used tea lights that we had taken from my mother's office. We lit the candles, and the air was still so they weren't immediately going out or anything. One strange thing we did notice is that as soon as our fingers hit the planchette, the forest seemed to go very quiet, and very still, suddenly. It freaked us out a little bit but again, it wasn't something that we were going to allow to deter us. We were frightened but excited and we giggled the whole time. At first, we asked if anyone was there, and the planchette immediately moved to the word "good-bye." That happened three times, but we didn't take the hint and continued trying to get something to communicate with us. We asked for the fourth time if anyone was there and the planchette moved to "yes." I knew Emily wasn't moving it and she knew that I wasn't, and we both immediately took our hands off the board. We were scared and both of us had a bad feeling. Still though, we pressed on. After a few minutes of establishing a connection, a spirit came through that claimed to be my grandfather. He had recently passed, and it had been very hard on me. He and I were super close and losing him had devastated me. I was in tears as I asked questions that only he would know the answers to and every single time the board, which I thought my grandfather was communicating with me through from beyond the grave, knew all the right answers.

This went on for about five minutes, the exchange with my "grandfather." Suddenly things started to get very scary. A very strong gust of wind came out of nowhere in the otherwise calm and windless night. It didn't only blow the candles out completely, but it sent two of them flying into the woods like they were made of feathers instead of hard wax and a metal base. At the same time, the planchette flew off the board and hit a nearby tree. We heard growling coming from somewhere in the woods, very close to us, right when the wind stopped blowing and the candles and planchette had landed. We didn't scream because honestly at that point we were more scared of our families catching us than we were of what we thought could have just been a little series of strange coincidences. We were both shaking and once the growling stopped, I started to giggle. I giggled and laughed a lot when I was very nervous and didn't know what else to do. Emily was giggling too, but I think she was doing it more to try and calm herself down. We decided to collect the candles and the planchette and hide the board in the woods. We knew we were supposed to get it to say "goodbye" before stopping the session with it, but we were inexperienced and decided to just ditch the board in the woods and get rid of the candles. I got up to collect the candles and told Emily to collect the board and planchette. She was reluctant and instead said she would keep watch to make sure no one from our families was coming close to us so that we didn't get caught. I hadn't thought of that and so I agreed to just collect everything and put it all into my bag. We were going to walk further into the woods, just a little bit, and hide everything. When we left to go home, we would just leave it there. Whatever we conjured that night, which wasn't my dearly departed grandfather, had other plans for us though.

I told Emily to keep watch while I walked and hid everything. She agreed and was happy not to have to go further into the woods or even touch that board again. We were both filled with terror and instant regret about what we had done. We would make sure we prayed later to find forgiveness because we also felt very guilty for using the spirit board. That's what we called it back then by the way, a spirit board. I felt like I was being followed the entire time I was looking with my flashlight for a place to put the board and candles where we wouldn't accidentally come across it when walking around with our parents and siblings. I heard a growling sound and when I turned to look there were two sets of red eyes peering at me from behind the trees. I screamed and dropped everything right there where I stood. I ran back to tell Emily what had happened. I felt like something was running behind me the entire way and I could hear the growling right next to my ear as though whatever it was, it was almost right on top of me. Emily and I took a long time to calm down and we tried to pray but kept being scared by the growling and losing our concentration. We looked around and all we saw were the two sets of red eyes looking at us, but we didn't see what was attached to them at first. Eventually, I think from adrenaline alone, we both passed out. I woke up to Emily screaming and when I looked over at her she was being dragged around in her sleeping bag. I will never forget the look of terror in her eyes and on her face at that moment. I looked up and suddenly there was a gigantic shadow figure hovering over me as I laid there, helpless to help either myself or my friend. I tried to scream but nothing would come out. The entity had red eyes that exuded evil and malicious intent. It smelled like someone was burning their trash nearby, but I knew it was the entity itself. It had a hood over its head. Eventually a small shriek escaped my throat, and I was able to move again. I jumped up and ran over to my best friend and asked if she was okay. She said that she was but we both had scratches all over our legs and arms. She had tears in her sleeping bag as if a grizzly bear had swiped it or something. We didn't know what to do and were shocked when no one came running at the sounds of our screaming.

We put her sleeping bag back across from mine and just sat there, crying, and trying to comfort one another. Our scratches were bleeding a little bit, and later we saw they were only scrapes. As we sat there, we heard growling and the wind picked up again. Whatever was out there wasn't done with us yet. Two shadow beings, both about twelve or thirteen feet tall with red eyes and a shadowy hood walked out of the wilderness beyond where we were sitting. The hoods dropped from their heads and what we saw were the most grotesque and hideous beings or creatures we had ever seen. Their skin seemed like it was burning off their faces. They had green fangs for teeth and huge, puss filled globs all over their faces. They were slowly floating towards us, and it was almost like we were in one of the terrifying but very cheesy horror movies we loved to watch so much. It didn't take either one of us any consideration and we got up and ran to the campervan to tell our parents what had happened. In typical style of religious parents, they were only focused on the fact we had used the board and not anything else that we had been through. We got in so much trouble and once we were back home, we were both grounded for the entire summer. We also under-went something like an exorcism at church and honestly, I think that's what saved us from being haunted, hunted and overtaken by those two demons from hell that either dwelt in those woods already or who we summoned from the board. Maybe it was a little bit of both.

BEING a nurse in a retirement community was never an easy job. Every day was filled with challenges, from dealing with difficult patients to managing complex medical conditions. But despite the stress and long hours, I loved my job. It was rewarding to be able to make a difference in the lives of the elderly residents I cared for. My day would usually start early, with a quick breakfast and a cup of coffee before heading to work. When I arrived at the retirement community, I would check in with the other nurses and review the patients' charts to see if there were any changes in their conditions that needed attention.

Despite the challenges, there were also many moments of joy and laughter in my job. I loved hearing stories from the residents about their lives and experiences, and I enjoyed getting to know each of them on a personal level.

Overall, being a nurse in a retirement community was a challenging but rewarding job. It taught me the importance of compassion, patience, and understanding, and it gave me a new appreciation for the elderly and all they have to offer. It's important to note that I worked at a very high-end retirement community. We even had a courtyard where once a week we would have a controlled fire in the center of the huge elaborate court-yard where residents could mingle, sample wine, and even cook marshmallows. As all the residents would finish out the night, one of us would hang behind and watch the fire burn out and we could full douse it out.

I was working as a nurse in a retirement community when I first encountered the black-eyed children. It was a warm summer night, and I was sitting outside by the fire, enjoying the peace and quiet. That's when I heard the chime of the front door for visitors. Everyone else was busy and the fire was dying down. So, I got up to answer it, but when I looked through the peephole, I saw two children standing on the other side. They were both wearing old-fashioned clothes, and their eyes were completely black.

I felt a chill run down my spine as I opened the door. The children asked if they could come in and use the phone, but something about them made me uneasy. I don't know if it was the look of their hollowed-out face, the gray color of their skin or if it was the strange smell of decay. I remember gulping for air and telling them in a steady voice that I couldn't let them in and tried to close the door.

But that's when things got really strange. The children began to plead with me, begging me to let them in. Their voices were soft and eerie, and their eyes seemed to glow in the darkness. Even after I closed the door it was as if they could see me through the door. I backed away slowly. I tried to ignore them and went back to my seat by the campfire. But they didn't give up. They continued to knock on the door and beg me to let them in. I warned the others not to answer the door. As the night wore on, I began to feel like I was being watched. Every time I looked up, I saw the black-eyed children standing just out of reach of the light from the campfire.

Finally, I couldn't take it anymore. I went inside and locked all the doors and windows. But even then, I could still hear them knocking and pleading with me. I called the police to report two lost children at our door. But by the time they came. The children were gone. I left out the creepiness and saw them in the facility out. Because how the heck did, they get in the courtyard. It was closed in the courtyard! I called at the end of my shift to check if they ended up finding those children. Maybe I was exhausted and misinterpreted what happened. The last thing I needed was to be viewed as a nut bag or worse. What if someone had said I had been drinking on the job. I couldn't afford to get fired from this job. So, I decided to take the roundabout way.

The next day, I asked around about the black-eyed children, but no one had ever seen or heard of them before. It was like they had never existed.

From that day on, I never sat outside by the campfire again. I took any other option than being the last one standing late at night. And even though I never saw those children again, I always felt like they were watching me from somewhere in the darkness. I even switched to the morning shift just to be safe. Even to this day, I feel them lurking by. Weeks went by, and I tried to convince myself that it was just my imagination playing tricks on me. But every time I closed my eyes, I could see those black-eyed children staring back at me. I don't know what it is was they wanted but I most certainly did not want to find out.

One night, I woke up to the sound of scratching at my bedroom window. I got out of bed and cautiously approached the window. When I looked out, I saw the two children standing outside, their eyes still black as coal. I tried to scream, but no sound came out. The children continued to scratch at the window, and I could feel their presence growing stronger with each passing moment. Suddenly, the scratching stopped, and the children disappeared into the darkness. But even though they were gone, I knew that they would be back.

I couldn't take it anymore. I quit my job and moved away from the retirement community as fast as I could. But even now, years later, I still have nightmares about those black-eyed children and wonder if they're still out there, haunting someone else's dreams.

CHAPTER TWELVE_
DEMONS AT THE FAIRGROUNDS

I WAS BORN and raised in Alaska and specifically the area where I live is known for being either haunted, or having something else, something unknown very much wrong with it. It's a place where UFOs are constantly seen hovering or darting back and forth in the sky and where people tend to go missing for a little while, only to be found again and have no memory of what had happened to them or where they were. I've always been interested in the supernatural and paranormal and I spend a lot of my free time looking on the internet for real encounter stories of things that have happened to people that are terrifying or at the very least unexplainable. I recently came across several stories about a place, said to be in Alaska, that everyone was referring to as the fairgrounds. They talked about how it's haunted and has been for as long as anyone who was writing about it could remember. It dawned on me that more likely than not, those people are talking about an area that's located right in my hometown and that also just happens to be the place where I had my most terrifying encounter with something demonic. It's not uncommon for teenagers in the area or who attend the local high school to volunteer to work at the fairgrounds in the warmer months when there's a lot of activity there. I don't know what the grounds used to be used for but for as far back as I can remember it is the fair for a few months in the summer and then it goes back to being a creepy and unoccupied field that seems to serve no purpose at all but that you can get in a lot of trouble for if you're caught trespassing on it. My parents told me one time, a long time ago, that it's because the land itself is haunted and whenever someone would try and do something more permanent with the land, it would always end in some sort of tragedy. Even as a teenager it didn't make sense to me that they would then proceed to hold a yearly affair there with little kids and cheap scares in mind. It sounded like a myth or another old town legend to me because why would anyone risk the so-called danger of haunted or tainted land being a place for family fun. I digress though and when I was seventeen, I decided to work at the fair for the fourth year in a row. It would look good on my college applications and was considered as volunteer work. My two best friends were working there with me, and we all had the same schedule which worked out even better.

We knew a lot of the kids from our school would be there and that we wouldn't be able to hang out, but it wasn't like we were working every night. Little did we know that after the first night we would not only never go back to work there again but we never attended the fair and we never even went anywhere near the surrounding woods again either. In fact, I have since stayed out of the woods and away from that fair altogether ever since it happened, despite still living here almost thirty years later. If my kids want to go then they must go with their father or another adult, no exceptions. It's really affected my life because here in Alaska there isn't much more to do than hang out in the woods or spend time as a family camping, hiking, fishing, and hunting. It just isn't for me anymore after what my friends and I encountered that night. We were excited just to be able to hang out together and were of course talking about all the cute boys in our school who we thought would be there on opening night. We got a little more dolled up than usual and were put in charge of the pony rides and then general clean up once it closed for the night. That was a job specifically for older teenagers and adults because the woods surrounding the place could get scary at night and they could also be dangerous because of the wild animals. Not to mention, people are allowed to drink there, or they used to be back when I was a teenager and there were always the town creeps lurking in the woods with who knows what sort of intent.

We got through the first night without any sort of issues, but we couldn't wait to be done because we were invited to a little get together in the woods afterwards by some classmates. These young men and women were considered the popular kids, which me and my friends were not, and we were excited to have gotten the invitation. We had a curfew, but we knew that since our parents had agreed to let us walk home together, we would have at least a few minutes to stop and try to make a good impression on the popular kids. Our parents knew it wouldn't be until around two in the morning that we would be finishing up and that we would be cutting through the woods, but it was a different time then and things just didn't seem as dangerous back then. Their biggest concern was the wild animals and even as females we had been raised to know what to do if approached by one of them and how to handle ourselves.

We were good and trustworthy kids and so we knew that we would be perfectly fine. My friends were all going to stay the night at my house that night anyway so after the little gathering in the woods we would just rush home and go to sleep. It was unlikely my parents would have even been awake, except for my mom maybe sleeping on the couch to make sure we all got in okay. Anyway, it was finally time to clean up and the most popular boy and girl in school came up to us and told us where they would all be and that they had beer. They said they would only be there for about a half hour because they had curfews as well and so we needed to hurry. They didn't offer to help us with cleaning up or anything, so we hurried and got our work done in record time. My two best friends and I walked into the woods and started looking for the landmark the others had pointed out. It took us longer than expected to find it and once we got there, we were bummed that they weren't there anymore. We decided to go back to my house and call it a night, figuring the next night would be another opportunity. It was a thirty-minute walk through the woods to get to my house and we had walked it so many times throughout the years. We hung out in those same woods and the fairgrounds was near the high school we all attended so we would have to walk through them to get home from school as well sometimes.

We were just talking and trying to pay attention to where we were going. No matter how used to the woods we were, it was still the middle of the night and creepy out there. We heard what sounded like kids laughing, not little kids but kids our age, and we were excited. We thought that it was going to be the kids who invited us to hang out with them. We got off the trail a little bit and had to walk through the woods towards where we heard the sounds come from, but it wasn't a big deal, and we were confident that we would easily be able to find our way back onto the right trail again. We saw some boys about our age sitting on the stone wall in the middle of a clearing that we were very familiar with. They weren't facing us and seemed to be caught up in whatever they were laughing about at the time. Though we could only see them from behind, and even though we could see them clearly, we couldn't figure out who they were. There were three guys there and none of them looked familiar. It was their haircuts that stood out to us right away as ones we hadn't ever seen before. This haircut wouldn't become popular until sometime in the nineties and I always referred to it once it did become common as "the bowl cut." Every one of the guys we knew had mullets back then, unfortunately. Also, flannel wasn't that common among the youth back then and so when we noticed they were wearing flannel and what looked like baggy, ripped up jeans, we knew we didn't know who they were and shouldn't approach them, regardless of whether they were our age. I whispered very low to my friends that we needed to go back and shouldn't alert the young men to our presence but somehow, they heard us. They suddenly stopped laughing and talking and for a minute they just sat there. None of them were facing us up to that point. Then, they all turned around at once and looked right at us.

They had giant, abnormally large grins on their faces, all of them looking the same. That wasn't what was terrifying us though. What we immediately noticed was their eyes. I have read stories about the black-eyed kids, but this was something altogether different. These boys didn't have all black eyes like in that phenomenon but instead, there were just dark black voids where the eyes should have been. My friends and I screamed and started to run the other way. We heard the boys also scream but it sounded very animalistic and like a bunch of hyenas or something. We knew for a fact they were chasing us though none of us would dare turn around and look. We didn't continue through the woods but went to the fairgrounds where we knew there would be security guards there overnight and asked them if we could use the phone to call my parents. They saw we were upset but once we explained why they rolled their eyes and accused us of being drunk or stoned. I called my house and my dad answered and he could tell I was scared about something and headed right out to get us. As we waited for him my friends and I considered how the security guard had acted towards us when we told him our story and therefore decided not to tell anyone about it. We never did and only told my dad that we had seen some wild, predatory animal or another and that we had gotten scared to continue the path to our house. He said he understood and that was that. As an adult I talk about the story often and to anyone who will listen. We all know what we saw that night. It wasn't a trick of the light or the product of overactive imaginations. One thing I think about often is the fact that in the black-eyed kid phenomenon, they seem to almost always be dressed in out-of-date clothing. The clothes they wear are often from some far distant time in the past and it's obvious they don't belong almost immediately because of that fact. However, in the case of my experience with those entities that had black voids for eyes, they almost seemed to be dressed like they were from the future. They looked like kids straight out of the early to mid-nineties instead of kids from the eighties, which was when we saw them, or earlier. I don't know how that all comes into play, but it is something I think about often. I don't care who thinks I'm crazy and who believes me. I know what I saw. They were demons or something worse and I wholeheartedly believe they belonged somehow to those damn fairgrounds.

CHAPTER THIRTEEN_
ALIENS IN THE WOODS?

I'VE ALWAYS LOVED the great outdoors and spent most of my time growing up spending time out in nature for one reason or another. It kind of runs in my family and from a very young age I was being brought into one forest or another to go camping or hiking with my family. I'll admit that throughout the years I have seen, heard and otherwise experienced some very strange and sometimes terrifying things while I was out there exploring. However, the encounter I am writing about today is by far the most terrifying for me to even must sit here and remember and that's why I chose this incident to write about first. I come from a long line of family that believes not only in paranormal and supernatural things and happenings but who also believe in extraterrestrials and beings from other planets. Just like with anyone else, in my family what a person believes depends on who you ask and that person's personal experiences that they've had throughout their lives. Almost everyone in my family has had some sort of communication with extraterrestrials at some point in their lives and when I made it to the age of thirty without ever experiencing anything like that, I started to think that maybe it just wasn't going to happen for me. I can't say I was too disappointed because a lot of the experiences other members of my family have had with them haven't been the best or most uplifting experiences and they've been, for the most part at least, traumatizing and horrifying. It was all about to come to a head for me when I decided to go on a tour of a specific part of the Appalachian Trail that I won't mention here because I know how some people are and they will want to go to that exact spot, even though the tours are shut down now and I doubt the other person involved is still working around there anyway, and I don't want anyone else to go and put themselves in danger on account of my story. Therefore, I will be as vague as possible about exactly where I was and what I was doing. With that being said, I was camping out with a group of about twelve other people, none of whom I knew before arriving there, and we were all interested in a specific part of the forest along the Trail itself. It wasn't for any sort of otherworldly reason that we all shared this interest, and the tour wasn't paranormal in nature and had nothing to do with extraterrestrials.

The group of us were all camping in the middle of the forest and there were two guides who would be taking us through the tour and along the trails for our daily itinerary. The whole tour lasted about four days and I had planned on staying for a few extra days, to camp overnight by myself after it was all over. From the moment I got there I felt good about it. The people seemed like nice folks, and I had gone on similar tours in the past and had always had a lot of fun. I had a very particular interest that I knew was shared by these strangers and it sort of brought us together. Once we all got to talking to one another it was like we had all known each other our entire lives. We were all around the same age except for one young man who had come along with his mom. He was a good sport though and seemed happy enough to be there and spending some time with his mother. The two tour guides had led us to the campsite and from the moment I had left my own home two states away to take the drive to the meeting spot, everything had been perfectly fine and seemingly normal up to that point. The tour guides had a weird energy about them. I know that's a hard thing to understand but it's one of those things where if you know then you just know. It's like they were all smiles and happy go lucky but there was something about them that gave me the creeps. Obviously, I didn't ask anyone else if they got the same weird and somewhat negative vibes off the guides because I didn't want to be rude, insult our hosts or seem strange myself, but I couldn't shake the feeling that there was something very wrong with those two guides. Granted, I had no idea what in the world it was or why I was feeling that way, but I just didn't like them. However, I did my very best to suppress those strange and unexpected feelings that I was having and was determined to put it out of my mind to enjoy the very expensive tour I was taking for the next few days.

The first day we all just got settled and the guides broke us up into two groups of five and each of them took one group off on a hike to explore the area. There was one male guide and one female. I was with the group being led by the female guide and at first everything seemed normal. She spoke in a somewhat bored and monotone fashion and her laugh was so high pitched it literally pierced my ears. I felt them ring and got an immediate mini headache every time that woman would so much as giggle. It was very annoying but like I said I was really trying to just ignore it and focus on the trip itself and how fortunate I had been to have been able to get the time off work and to afford such a wonderful trip in the first place. I noticed the young man and his mother were in my group and I also noticed that he was not standing up front with his mom, but off to the side and behind everyone else, as far away from the guide as possible without him seeming rude. I went up to him and whispered, asking if everything was alright. He was a young teenager and therefore didn't care as much as I did about be rude, I guess because he came right out and told me the guide was giving him the creeps, but he just couldn't put his finger on it. He said she didn't seem human to him and was more like a robot. That struck me immediately and chilled me to my bone because while I hadn't been able to place exactly what my issues were with the woman; he had nailed it in that one sentence. She didn't seem real somehow. Who knows, if I hadn't grown up believing in the things I had, then maybe I would have laughed it off or thought that he was the strange one but as soon as he said that there was no going back, and I knew that something very odd and somewhat terrifying was going on with the tour guides. Not just the woman but both of them. We were walking to our next stop on the tour and me and the young man continued our conversation in a whisper as we walked. Once we stopped again and were told to go and explore on our own for a few moments, I noticed the tour guide glaring at me and him. There was no possible way she could have heard us but somehow, I knew that she had.

I smiled at her, and she immediately smiled back and that's when I noticed her lips looked fake, almost like they were only made of lipstick and there was nothing underneath. The boy went to find his mother and I went walking around the area, looking at all the beautiful scenery. I had a question and went up to the guide to ask her. I noticed right away, as soon as I had gotten within a few feet of her, that she smelled horribly. It was like a mixture of rotting flesh and embalming fluid. I used to visit my dad at work at a funeral parlor and knew the smell very well. There was no mistaking it and I knew that's what I was smelling the moment it hit my nose. I tried not to react to it because she was looking right at me, watching me walk up to her. I leaned in to show her something I had found and asked for her opinion on it. As she started explaining it to me, I just happened to look up at her face, which was mere inches from my own at that point. That's when it happened! I noticed her face looked different somehow and I could see that she was wearing a ton of makeup and the skin underneath was a bluish green color. I gasped even though I was trying so hard not to react, and she immediately looked up at me. That's when I saw that her ordinary brown eyes that I had noticed earlier in the day were now yellow and had slits like reptiles have. There's no possible way that a real human being could have eyes like that without putting contact lenses in. She had brown eyes when I initially walked up to her, so I knew that contacts were out of the question as far as any explanation was concerned. Her eyes only shifted for a split second or less, but I had been staring right at them and saw it as clearly as I could see the rest of the people and the wilderness around me.

I backed up a little bit as she blinked and suddenly her eyes were brown again. They looked perfectly normal, if not a little big in proportion to her very human looking head. I noticed she had on a ratty black wig too and it was crooked and matted in places. As soon as I thought about the wig, her hand went to her head and she adjusted it, all the while looking me in the eyes. She winked at me and licked her lips, revealing a strange, forked tongue. I know it sounds insane but believe me I know what I saw. The forked tongue didn't last either because I had noticed her earlier in the day when she was speaking to the male tour guide, I caught a glimpse of her tongue. It wasn't even something I had been aware of until that moment. I backed away from her without saying another word and didn't look in her direction for the remainder of that portion of the tour. Once dusk settled over the forest, we all headed back to the camp to have some dinner and settle in for the night. We built a large campfire and as we did, I noticed the tour guides were huddled in a little corner of the camp, having a very heated discussion about something. I strained to try and hear what they were talking about but as soon as I started trying to listen harder, they both looked up at me and stopped talking. They walked over to the campfire and suggested we tell some scary stories. Everyone except for me and the teenage boy thought it was a great idea and most of the others seemed delighted by it. We all dutifully sat around the large fire and listened as the two guides told some scary story about an evil reptilian race who had infiltrated human society and who lived in the woods amongst the trees and other animals. They said the race had big plans for humanity and that they survived by eating the animals in the wilderness and occasionally, they would take an unsuspecting human. This all happened right around the time when the missing people in the woods started to become more of a noticeable thing. However, I guess most of the people there weren't aware of all of that because they laughed and chuckled as the guides did the same and finished up their terrifying story. At the end everyone was amused and some of them even clapped. I noticed the teenager looked terrified and seemed all but amused with the story. I wasn't too thrilled either.

I barely slept that night and left the tour as soon as the sun came up the very next day. I've questioned what happened to me so many times throughout the last few years and I often wonder if my mind had been playing tricks on me or something. There are other times though, often, and normally when it's silent and dark in my bedroom at night, that I know what I had really seen was the truth and that I had encountered some sort of extraterrestrial that shapeshifted into a human or something like that. I don't pretend to know how it all works but I do think wholeheartedly that the scary campfire story the two of them told was based in reality, at least somewhat. Who knows if they used that job to find victims or if they were just hiding in plain sight and not actually doing anything nefarious at all. I also wonder if that's the reason those tours were shut down because I haven't been able to find anything online about why it isn't running anymore and can only see that it isn't. It was a tour that had been going on for at least three decades up until a year after I had my experience on it. I honestly don't know what to think and I have had a few more experiences with the same type of fake human creature ever since when I hadn't ever had any sort of experiences like it up to that point. I've discussed it with my parents and other members of my family, and they believe my initial evaluation of the situation and that I encountered alien infiltrators. It terrifies me so much thinking about how many of those things could be out there, just living lives as though they are normal human beings and victimizing who knows how many unsuspecting victims while they're at it. I am more careful than ever before when out in the woods nowadays and ever since I had that terrifying experience, but it didn't stop me from wandering around out there altogether. I often wonder if they knew I knew about them and if that's why I have seen them so many times since. I have so many questions and almost no answers and the answers I do have are based on my own theories and speculation but that doesn't mean none of it is rooted in fact and in fact it means only that it can't yet be proven.

CHAPTER FOURTEEN_

GRAVEYARD GHOUL

Whenever I tell people about my encounter, I get one of two reactions. Either they are terrified and super interested in all the details and my thoughts about what happened to me, or they think I am insane or trying to play some sort of strange trick on them and aren't sure what to say about any of it. One thing I do know is that what I saw was real and it happened to me. I have always been a big believer in the paranormal and it kind of runs in my family. I grew up with parents who weren't very religious and a mother who loves horror movies. The first movie I ever remember watching was a horror movie and I even asked to have the main character from that incredibly horrifying and scary movie on my cake and at my party when I turned four. That just goes to show how into all that kind of stuff I am. It got to the point though where I just stopped talking about my experience because I couldn't take people not believing me anymore and I was starting to gain a reputation as either a liar or a loser, depending on what the person making that assessment initially thought when I told them what I had endured that night. My encounter happened in the woods of Alabama, in the middle of an old and abandoned cemetery, in 1976. I was seventeen years old and didn't have a care in the world up to that point.

My best friend and I were having a sleepover at my house like we always did on Friday nights and as usual we got bored right around midnight. We didn't drink or do drugs at all, and we didn't have many friends aside from one another. We watched a few horror movies and decided to go for a walk in the woods to this tiny, abandoned cemetery from the fifteen hundreds or something like that. We spent a lot of time there and with the way that my room was set up we didn't have to worry about getting caught sneaking out. Plus, it wasn't unusual for us to run to the store at all hours of the night to get some snacks for another horror movie marathon, so we really wouldn't have gotten in much trouble anyway. Maybe my dad would have lectured us about being out so late at night but that would have been the extent of it. Anyway, we were bored and normally when that happened, we would walk through the woods that surrounded my house and go to the cemetery. One of the things we liked to do there was take random pictures in the dark, using the flash, and then once they were developed try and see if we caught any ghosts or demons, things like that, on the film. It wasn't like nowadays where you just take out your phone and snap a photo or shoot a video and it took almost a week to get film developed. Also, you didn't get to see the photos beforehand so maybe one or two pictures out of every roll of twenty-four would be worth keeping. There were also no filters. I know, it's hard to imagine but that's how it was. The photos don't mean anything though because they aren't really a part of the encounter except that's what we had planned on doing when we headed out towards the cemetery in the woods.

We realized right before we left that neither one of our cameras had any film, so we had to run to a nearby all night convenience store and grab some. Because we were driving to the cemetery and not walking through my backyard, the route we were taking was a little different. The space was open enough, the way it was all set up, so that my little Volkswagen fit perfectly through the trails. We grabbed a few things from the store, including the film, and went on about our business. By the time we got to the cemetery it was almost one in the morning. We exited the car and sat on one of the benches. We loaded the film into our cameras using the lights inside so that we didn't have to fumble around with it in the dark or by light of the only two, very small and barely illuminating flashlights we had with us. It started off as very normal and average for us and we were just goofing around, minding our own business, and snapping random photos of one another and random areas in the graveyard that "felt weird" to us. We hadn't ever caught anything on any images, and we had taken thousands of photos there by that point in time. We were just sitting on the bench and had been there for about twenty minutes when we both suddenly got the chills and started feeling scared. It seemed like it had come on for no reason and when I mentioned it to her, she said she felt like something was watching us from the woods or something. I felt it too and told her so. Normal people would have gotten the hell out of there right then but then again "normal people" wouldn't have driven to a graveyard in the middle of the night to snap photos of ghosts and demons because they were bored either, I suppose.

We decided to snap some more photos, enough to at least run out the rolls of film that were in the cameras already, before leaving and heading back to my house. We were being silly but there was an underlying and unmentioned sense of fear and dread that colored the atmosphere and we both felt it very deeply. Just as the flash went off as I snapped my last photo of the night, we both heard a very low growling sound coming from just beyond where we were able to see from where we were sitting. We both turned at the same time and asked one another if we had heard that. Once we heard it again, she turned and started walking quickly back to the car, but I needed to see what it was. As girls who were born and raised in the country, we were both very familiar with all the wildlife out in those woods at the time and we both knew it wasn't anything we had ever heard before or were aware of. A part of me was excited because this was exactly what we had gone out there for in the first place after all, right? We wanted to contact the spirit realm, and I knew without a doubt that somehow, we had managed to do just that. I called for her to come with me, but I could see she was terrified and trying not to cry. I mocked her a little bit to get her to go with me to see what was making those horrible sounds. Finally, she relented and stormed over to me. We both turned our flashlights on and walked towards the tree-line, where it was pitch black, and where we couldn't see anything at all from where we were. I wish we had never gone out there that night or at the very least I wish that I had followed her back to the car the moment we heard whatever the growling noises were. It occurred to us that maybe it was other teenagers or some other human being who had noticed us out there, snapping photos and talking about ghosts and demonic entities, who then decided to try and play a prank to scare us. That thought not only calmed us down a lot, but it also made us a lot more brazen. We yelled into the darkness, asking in unison who was out there but we only heard more growling in response.

I should mention here that every single one of the tombstones and grave markers were nothing more than piles of busted cement and rubble at that point. When we approached the noise after considering it was someone trying to scare us, we didn't want to shine our lights right in the person's face because who knows if it was some psychopathic killer or a homeless person wanting to rob us or worse. Better to not make them angry even more just in case. We aimed our lights in front of us but on the ground and we both stopped short the second we realized what was in front of us. It was a fully intact gravestone that wasn't broken or even eroded at all. We slowly shined our lights up to the top of it from where they were facing on the ground and that's when we saw what we thought was someone just sitting there. They weren't facing us, but we could see a little bit of the side of them, and it looked like they were sitting there, on top of the gravestone, with what we call nowadays "pretzel legs" but what we called back then "Indian style." Basically, they were sitting with their legs crossed in front of them. They looked like they had a dark blanket wrapped around their shoulders that covered their back and arms, along with most of the rest of their body and they had an extremely pale, bald head. We just stopped and kept our lights trained on the person. "Hello?" I asked timidly. Suddenly and without warning the "person" jumped up so that they were standing on top of the head stone.

It took less time than it did for me to blink once for them to turn, stand up and fling the blanket to the ground. The person, or whatever it was, moved at super-human speeds. I kept my light trained on them as my friend turned and ran, screaming for dear life as she went. She screamed for me to follow her but as much as my brain was telling me to go with her and get the hell out of there, my legs felt like they were frozen to the ground. I couldn't move my arms either and kept my light trained right on that thing. It growled and shrieked, and it felt like my ears would bleed. It was so shrill and horrible sounding. It bared its teeth at me, and I could see it had jagged yellow fangs and what looked like blood all over its mouth. Well, where the mouth should have been because honestly, and I've thought about this a lot over the years, it looked like it chewed its own mouth off. I don't know why I thought that, but I remember that I did, and it's never left me. It had the skinniest body I had ever seen and wasn't much taller than me. I was five foot and six inches tall, but it was still standing on top of the head stone. It growled again. It looked like it had no nose and every single bone in its body was popping out and looked like it was just about to rip right through the skin. The skin, by the way, was gray and looked like it was wet. It glistened in the moonlight. The eyes were all black and I can't be sure anymore, but I didn't think it had any eyelids or eyelashes. It had no eyebrows either and in fact was seemingly completely bald. That was all I was able to see before it leapt down off the tombstone and took off running after me. I was no longer paralyzed, and my adrenaline must have kicked in. It was running so incredibly fast I have no idea how I got away from it. I barely made it to the car and got the door shut and locked before it was right up almost on top of me. It started banging on the sides of the car and I remember being terrified it would bust the windows out with nothing but sheer strength if I didn't get us out of there.

My best friend was screaming and crying, begging me to get us away from it. I yelled that I was trying. We heard a loud thump on the roof as I got the engine started and peeled out of there as fast as I could. I slammed on the brakes, and it went flying into the middle of the road up ahead of us but before I even started moving again it had leapt through the air and was aiming, or so I thought, to land back on the roof again. I don't know if it missed or what happened, but it didn't land on the car. We didn't see it again and just kept driving until we got back to my house. We were shaken and terrified, but we had the presence of mind to be quiet and not wake anyone up. Our lives ever since have been filled with everything I mentioned in the beginning of this encounter as far as always trying to judge who to tell and who out of those we do tell will believe us. I don't know what it was except to maybe say it was a ghoul or perhaps some sort of demon. I don't even know if they're one and the same. I've never been back there, and I have avoided the woods at nighttime at all costs ever since. I don't even go to funerals anymore and stay as far away as humanly possible, under all circumstances, from cemeteries. There were no strange pictures on either roll of film. Thanks for letting me share this with the world.

CONTINUE WITH
TALES OF TERROR, VOLUME 2

ABOUT THE AUTHOR_

Ethan Hayes grew up in Oklahoma and moved to Texas when he attended Texas A&M. Upon graduation he was hired by Texas Parks and Wildlife and remained there until he retired twenty-two years later. He currently lives in southeast Texas with his wife and two dogs. When he's not spending time enjoying the outdoors and writing, he sips a cold beer on his front porch while listening to Bluegrass music.

Send in your encounter story:
encountersbigfoot@gmail.com

ALSO BY ETHAN HAYES_

Grab these other great Free Rein Publishing Books.

STAT: Bizarre Medical Stories

Get

STAT: Bizarre Medical Stories

www.ingramcontent.com/pod-product-compliance
Lightning Source LLC
Chambersburg PA
CBHW052005170626
46808CB00007B/2786